W9-CIB-225

Foreword Indies Book of the Year Finalist

National Indie Excellence Finalist

USA Best Books Finalist

*To my friend*

# The Life and Rhymes of Miss Biscuit

## "Lost and Found"

*Biscuit*

*Jason*

## Jason Phinney

## Illustrated by Jessica Mattea Dupree

Copyright 2016 Jason Phinney

Lenny Paws Publishing

All rights reserved.

ISBN 13: 9780996942805

I'm not certain who I am
I wasn't called a name
At least one I remember
By those from which I came

To wander down lonely streets
Hoping to find some food
Why they left me here alone
I never understood

Shivering with soaking fur
Paws tired and in pain
I snuck into a woodshed
To shelter from the rain

I laid my head upon a pile
Of mulch strewn on the floor
And slept with one eye open
Then saw him at the door!

A large and fearsome canine
With fur of brown and black
If I didn't mind my manners
He looked like he'd attack!

"Who said that you could sleep here?
I'd really like to know
This can't be your place to live
You best get up and go"

"Kind sir, I beg your pardon
There's no cause for alarm
I have nowhere else to go
Please share with me your farm"

"You had better get on up
And get on down the lane
If the owner finds you here
We'll both be in the rain

I work here as a guard dog
So I can't take a chance
And risk the food he throws me
When I go beg and dance"

So I gathered up my courage
And headed for the door
His gentle paw restrained me
He'd thought of one thing more

"If you can keep real quiet
I'll share some food with you
I know I might regret it
But what else can I do?"

He led me to the horse barn
Past bales and bales of hay
Left me in an empty stall
Returning soon to say

"Have some of these snacks right here
They're biscuits from last week"
I swallowed down three ones whole
Before I took a peek

And noticed he was watching
A tear welled in his eye
I asked what was the matter
That made a big dog cry

He said never had he seen
A skinny thing like me
A coat so dull and worn out
And ribs all plain to see

"I guess I'll call you Biscuit
The way you wolfed them down
The folks here call me Buddy
When they want me to come 'round"

He told me I could hide away
In the horse stall near the back
And if the owner walked that way
He'd get the ducks to quack

To warn me they were coming
So no one would find out
He'd try to find some extra food
The roadside he would scout

Then Buddy introduced me
To his friend Simone Raccoon
Asking her to care for me
So I'd feel better soon

"Why yes I'll help this little girl
Although I must confess
She looks so weak and skinny
Her coat is such a mess!

It's brittle and it's dirty
In places it's not there
I hope that I can salvage
A little of her hair"

"I'll wash and brush your tattered coat

To make it look real nice

Dear you need some weight on you!

We'll have to feed you twice!


Now sit right down, I'll fix you up

Your health will come along

Each day you'll feel much better

You'll sing a brand new song"

With lessons from Simone

I learned how to behave

The times to be real cautious

And when I should be brave


She showed me how to forage

Through garbage cans at night

Then taught me how to spell my name

And how to read and write

Buddy took me hunting
He showed me all the ropes
So I could be a partner
And help the pack to cope

Because we had sparse rations
We'd have to find some prey
And share the catch between us
To make it through each day

Then one day a car appeared
And parked along the street
A man got out, looked my way
Then left a tasty treat!

For me, Simone, and Buddy
To eat and get our fill
We eagerly awaited
The long, cold hours 'til

He again returned at dawn
Delivering more food
We filled up then ate some more
It brightened up our mood!

Each morning he arrived here
As weeks and weeks went by
My body grew much stronger
My spirit learned to fly

The hunting trips were cancelled
The garbage raids were done
No longer did we struggle
The time had come for fun

Bellies full we ran and played
Chased ducks across the pond
Happy times we shared each day
Made stronger our deep bond

I was so very lucky
My Buddy took me in
I never would've made it
Alone and cold and thin

A little act of kindness
Can sometimes be enough
To turn around another's life
When times have gotten tough

My days have been much brighter
With my Buddy and Simone
Because we're all together
I will never feel alone

Miss Biscuit grew up on a small farm near Chappell Hill, Texas. She learned the art of poetry from Simone Raccoon and has since written several stories that tell of her journey from hard times to happiness. She is currently on a sabbatical from writing and spends her time chasing squirrels and possums, sun bathing, and wrestling with her favorite playmate, Lady Daisy.

Jessica Dupree is an artist and children's book illustrator from Houston, Texas. She has a great love for all animals and enjoys painting and drawing them. She couldn't help falling in love with Biscuit and hopes you will too!

Jason Phinney was inspired to write children's books when a skinny dog named Biscuit joined his family and related the story of her life. Impressed by her literary skills, Jason wanted to share her heartwarming poetry with children everywhere.
To learn more, please visit Jasonphinney.com

62674808R00019

Made in the USA
Lexington, KY
15 April 2017